Leapfrog
World Tales

Issun Boshi

A Japanese tale
told by Mick Gowar

Illustrated by Cosei Kawa

W

FI   S

First published in 2009 by
Franklin Watts
338 Euston Road
London
NW1 3BH

Franklin Watts Australia
Level 17/207 Kent Street
Sydney
NSW 2000

A CIP catalogue record for this book is available
from the British Library.

ISBN 978 0 7496 8595 9 (hbk)
ISBN 978 0 7496 8601 7 (pbk)

Series Editor: Jackie Hamley
Series Advisor: Dr Barrie Wade
Series Designer: Peter Scoulding

Printed in China

Franklin Watts is a division of
Hachette Children's Books,
an Hachette UK company.
www.hachette.co.uk

This tale comes from Japan. Can you find Japan on a map?

This is the story of
Issun Boshi, which means
Little One.

He was a tiny boy,
no taller than me.

Issun Boshi was very brave, even though he was little.

4

"I'm going to see the world and be a soldier," he told his mother.

"I will see the world in my boat, and I will guard the Emperor with my sword!" he cried.

7

Issun Boshi rowed to
the Emperor's castle.

8

"Open the gate!" shouted Issun Boshi. "I've come to guard the Emperor!"

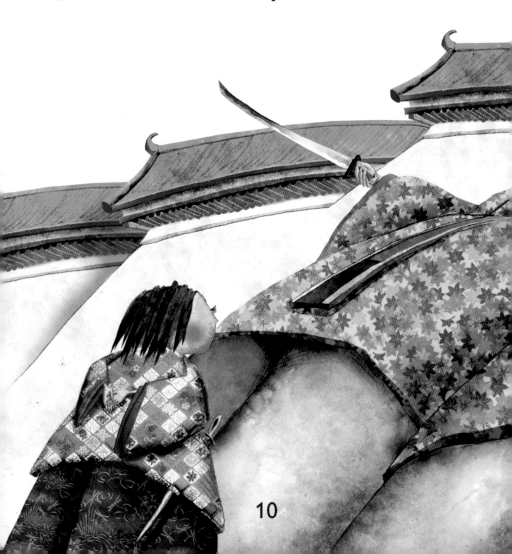

The soldiers laughed, but
they let Issun Boshi in.

"I wish you were as tall as you are brave!" said the Emperor.

"You will be my daughter's playmate."

"You can live in my doll's house," said the princess.

"And I will guard you," said Issun Boshi.

One day, a wicked ogre came to the castle. He waved his magic hammer.

The soldiers were very frightened. They ran away.

"I will be king!" the ogre told the princess. "And you will be my queen!"

"Never!" shouted
the princess.

"I'll save you, princess!"
cried Issun Boshi, pricking
the ogre's ear with
his sword.

"Ow!" cried the ogre. "An invisible soldier! Your magic is too strong for me!"

The ogre ran off, dropping his magic hammer. Issun Boshi fell to the ground.

"Get the hammer and make a wish!" whispered Issun Boshi, too hurt to move.

"Make Issun Boshi better," wished the princess.

24

"And make him as tall as he is brave!"

The princess married the tall, brave soldier, but she still called him ...

... Issun Boshi – Little One!

Puzzle 1

a

b

c

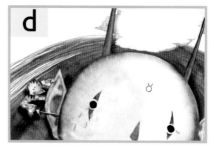

d

e

f

Put these pictures in the correct order.
Now tell the story in your own words.
What different endings can you think of?

Puzzle 2

brave   bold

fearful

sweet   tiny

frightening

kind   selfish

gentle

Choose the correct adjectives for each character. Which adjectives are incorrect? Turn over to find the answers.

Answers

Puzzle 1

The correct order is: 1c, 2e, 3b, 4d, 5f, 6a

Puzzle 2

Issun Boshi: the correct adjectives are bold, brave

The incorrect adjective is fearful

The ogre: the correct adjective is frightening

The incorrect adjectives are sweet, tiny

The princess: the correct adjectives are gentle, kind

The incorrect adjective is selfish

Look out for Leapfrog fairy tales: